COCOA BEACH LIBRARY
3 2480 00042 9056

W9-AEF-190

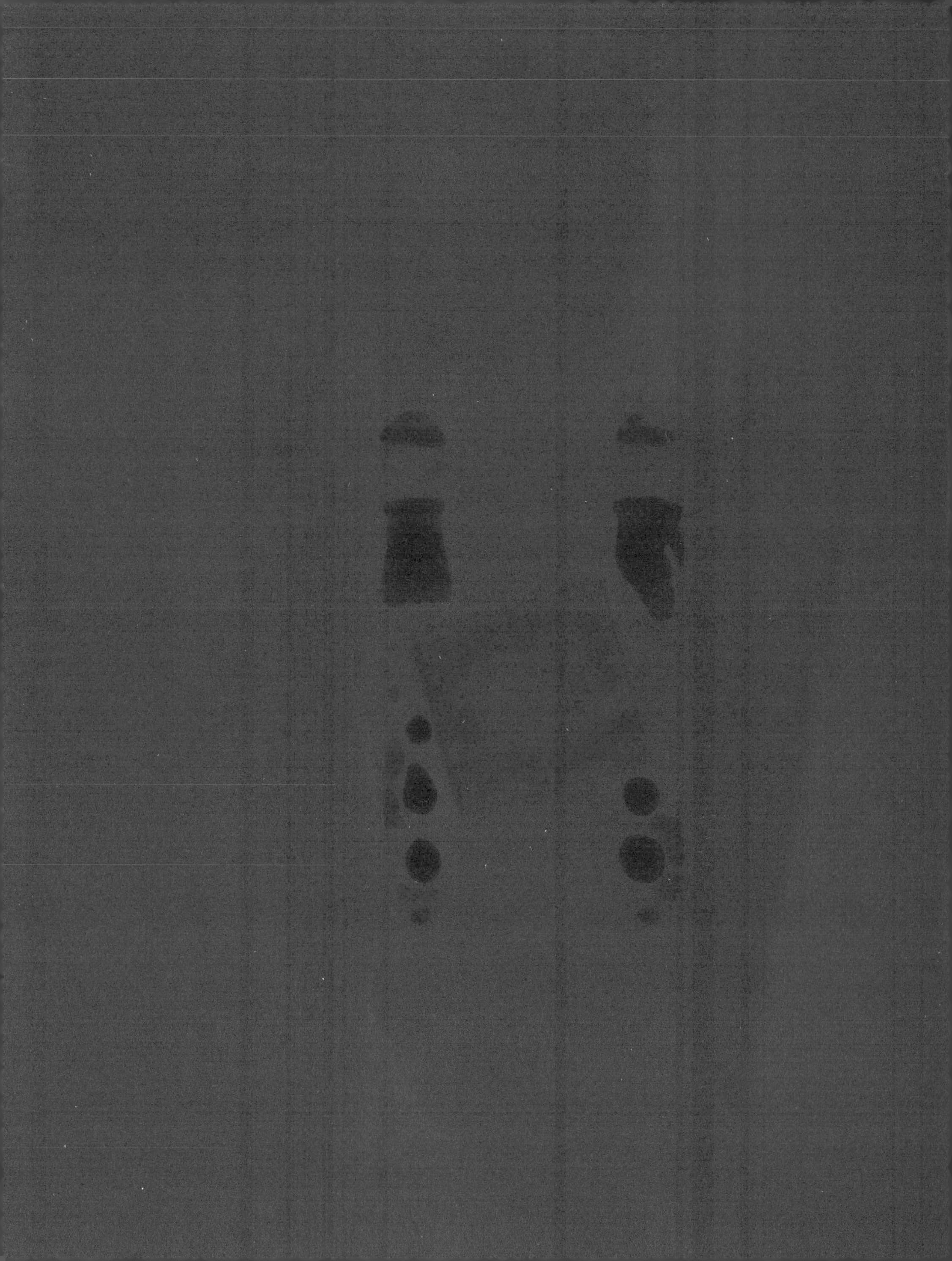

Song for the ANCIENT FOREST

Song for the ANCIENT FOREST

by NANCY LUENN
illustrated by JILL KASTNER

Atheneum 1993 New York

Maxwell Macmillan Canada
Toronto
Maxwell Macmillan International
New York Oxford Singapore Sydney

A Lucas/Evans Book

Atheneum. Macmillan Publishing Company
866 Third Avenue, New York, NY 10022
Maxwell Macmillan Canada, Inc., 1200 Eglinton Avenue East,
Suite 200, Don Mills, Ontario M3C 3N1
Macmillan Publishing Company is part of the
Maxwell Communication Group of Companies.

First edition
Printed in Hong Kong by South China Printing Company (1988) Ltd.
1 2 3 4 5 6 7 8 9 10

Library of Congress Cataloging-in-Publication Data

Luenn, Nancy. Song for the ancient forest/by Nancy Luenn; illustrated by Jill Kastner. —1st ed. p. cm. Summary: Raven warns against the destruction of the ancient forests, but no one listens except for a small child.
ISBN 0-689-31719-0 [1. Old growth forests—Fiction. 2. Forests and forestry—Fiction. 3. Forest conservation—Fiction.] I. Kastner, Jill, ill. II. Title.
PZ7.L9766So 1992 [E]—dc20 91-17187

For Glenn,
may your song be heard
N. L.

For Laura,
Jeremiah, and Dylan
J. K.

Long ago, before people came to walk beneath the big trees of the ancient forest, Raven lived there. Raven was a trickster. His harsh voice boasted of the tricks he played. He teased the other animals and stole their food, but he was also very wise.

One night, Raven had a dream. He dreamed that the forest was gone. Streams ran brown and the salmon died. The owl's song was no longer heard.

Raven awoke with a cry. He asked the world for a song to sing, a song of power that would change his dream.

The world's spirit answered. "Every song must have a singer. And each singer must find one who understands his song."

That is easy, thought proud Raven, for I am a great singer. He listened carefully while the spirit taught him his song.

When Raven grew tired of playing tricks on the other animals, he created a people from warm brown spring earth. They lived in the forest, cutting the trees they needed to build lodges and carve totem poles and shape canoes.

They gathered huckleberries in cedar baskets and fished for salmon in the autumn streams.

Raven stole their food and played tricks on them, but they honored him as their creator and welcomed him beside their fires.

When his belly was full, Raven would call out, "Listen!" He would tell of his frightening dream and sing his song.

The people laughed. "Oh, that is Raven just playing tricks

again," they said. They did not believe his dream. For they could not imagine a land without the forest.

Then Raven became angry. He made fir cones tumble from the sky until they fell like rain. Still, he went back the next evening, to eat and play his tricks and sing again.

Years passed like salmon swimming upstream. A new kind of people came into the land. They cut down trees to build their homes and cleared the forest for their farms. They pushed the first people away from their land.

The settlers cut more trees and began to sell their timber. "Listen!" Raven shouted to them, and he sang his song. But the

settlers did not understand him. All they heard was the call of a raven. When he stole their food, they did not laugh but drove him away.

Raven was very discouraged. Hiding, he pondered what the spirit had told him. *Every song must have a singer. And each singer must find one who understands his song.* But what if no one would listen?

More and more of the ancient trees fell. A day came

when the owl's song was seldom heard. The noise of buzzing saws and rumbling logging trucks disturbed the air. Only scattered patches of the ancient forest remained. Still, Raven sat in his tree, looking for the one who would understand his song.

Every day, a girl named Marni walked deep into the forest. She sat and listened to the murmur of the trees. Raven watched Marni with a hopeful eye.

One day she settled under Raven's tree. Silently, he drifted down. "I am Raven," he said proudly.

"Raven," whispered Marni, "how did you learn to talk?"

"I am Trickster," he boasted. "I *invented* talking."

Then he shouted, "Hah! You understand me!" No one had listened to Raven for years. Maybe she would even understand his song. Puffing out his feathers, Raven sang.

Marni listened and her face became grave. All day she sat in thought.

Then she went home and pleaded with her father. "Papa, we must stop cutting down our ancient forest."

Her father shook his head. "Marni," he said, "I am a logger. How will I make a living if I don't cut trees?"

"The trees do not *belong* to us, Papa. We belong to the forest." She sang him Raven's song in words she hoped he would understand.

Her father was silent, for he knew the ancient forest well. "Marni," he said finally, "let me think on this awhile."

He thought for many days, and each day his thoughts grew deeper. Perhaps his daughter was right. What would their future be without the forest?

At last he gathered the loggers together.

"Friends," he said. "We must stop logging the ancient forest."

"How will we make money?" they demanded. "What will we eat? How will we build homes? There are plenty of trees."

"But not much forest. Listen!" He sang Raven's song. "We must find a new way of logging, one that does not destroy the land. We can still cut trees, but let the ancient forest stand." Then he told them of his plan. A few agreed to try.

Together, they spoke to the man who owned the trees.

"We have always cut these trees," the owner argued. "Why should we stop now?"

Marni's father and his friends began singing Raven's song.

Raven, very proud of himself, sang loudest of all. But all the angry owner could hear was a raven calling *kraaw, kraaw.*

"Pesky bird!" He picked up a stone and threw it, hitting Raven.

Raven tumbled out of the tree and onto the ground, a heap of broken feathers. As he lay there, he felt his blood watering the earth.

With it his song flowed into the forest, and into every living thing.

Then the trees themselves began to sing!

When they heard the forest singing, the owner and his crew dropped their saws. For a moment they stood listening, mouths wide open. Then, terrified, they ran away.

Raven, dying, looked inside his bag of tricks. He found a

new suit of feathers. Leaving the old ones on the ground, he flew to a branch in a hemlock tree. He could feel it singing beneath him. The song carried life from the tips of his talons to his shiny new wings. He preened his feathers.

"Every song must have a singer," he told the world. "And *this* singer has found the one who understands his song!"

Then Raven opened his beak and sang.

Squirrel drops fungus in the forest
hemlock, cedar, spruce and fir
fungus growing, feeds the tree roots
starting round the circle of time

Fungus feeds squirrel, squirrel feeds owl,
marten, bobcat, fisher and mink
dying deer feeds wolf, and cougar
death feeds life in the circle of time

Spawning salmon feeds the eagle
cedar, bear and humankind
forest fills streams until autumn
fish come home in the circle of time

Dying tree falls, settles slowly
moss and seedlings grow on its spine
reaching up toward rain and sunlight
starting over, the circle of time

Without the squirrel there is no owl
without the salmon, eagle dies
without the fungus there is no forest
without the forest, no circle of time,
no circle of time, no circle of time. . . .